They met on the vine
on a warm, sunny day,
just hanging around
the way grapes
like to play.

Gretchen
and Gary Grape
became friends
on the vine
and chatted about
what they'd become
in due time.

Grape Grower Grady overheard them talking while, through the vineyard, he and Rover were walking.

"Well, little grapes," he said to the two, "when you finally leave the vine, there's a lot you can do."

"One choice is to become fresh grapes at the store for fruit bowls and salads and snack plates and more.

A grape tastes so good when it's plump, ripe and sweet.
There's no other fruit that's more fun to eat."

"You can also choose to dry-up off the vine until you're a raisin which tastes very fine.

Your skin must be shriveled and your pulp fun to chew. If you're a raisin there's a choice for you, too."

"Some come in snack boxes, ready to eat.
In salads and stuffing they sure are a treat.

Coleslaw with raisins makes a meal just great,
and raisin bran cereal helps maintain a healthy weight!"

"Grape seed cooking oil is another thing to be.
Instead of burning food on the stove,
it's golden brown that we see.

Nothing's better for making chicken, pasta or even stew. Grape seed oil is perfect in a lot of bakery, too."

"Plus, Gretchen and Gary, here's something kind of funny: grape seed oil's in lotions that cost a lot of money. It's used to put on sunburned skin to take the sting away so kids can go outside again to jump and run and play.

And then there's good old grape juice, a favorite drink for all -- in boxes, cans and bottles at every food store in the mall. It's usually dark grape color, but sometimes white juice, too. Every mom knows it's a hit with kids and is also good for you."

"Of course, you can choose to be a favorite of the belly, that all-time hit with everyone, sweet and smooth grape jelly.

A spoonful of jelly over soft peanut butter is a sure way to set any kid's heart aflutter."

"It's great for filled donuts or over whole wheat toast. Some dads even use it when they barbeque a roast.

And kids always try to be the last to leave the room, so they can be the lucky one who licks the jelly spoon."

"Now vinegar's another thing
a grape can plan to be.
It's used in things that are kind of sour
and some too tart for me.

You'll find vinegar in pickle juice, salad dressings and...

ketchup poured on all the food at every hotdog stand."

"Now, Gretchen and Gary, while you're thinking of what to be, consider the soil in which you grow and the name of your family.

Think of the sunshine
you enjoy each day
at noon,
and the cool evening
breezes that

come with the moon."

It means you could become a gold medal winner for grown-ups to enjoy with their favorite snack or dinner."

"Yes, little grapes, there is so much you could do. But, for special grapes it's wine, and that means both of you.

You'll age and mellow in barrels for a while… then enjoy the pleasure of a taster's approving smile!"

"Thanks, Grape Grower Grady," said Gretchen and Gary. "It's so nice to be a special grape, not just another berry!"